The Resurrection Tour Diaries

The Shooting Star Series

Simon Northouse

Flabbergasted Publishing

Published by Flabbergasted Publishing

First Edition

e-Book ISBN-13: 978-0-6482884-5-9

Paperback ISBN-13: 978-0-6482884-6-6

About The Author

Simon Northouse is the author of:

The Shooting Star series

The Soul Love series

The School Days series

Let's Get Discombobulated Newsletters Series

Contact Info

If you wish to contact the author then email:

simon@simonnorthouse.com

To subscribe to his monthly newsletter follow this link:

Simon Northouse - The Discombobulated Newsletter

If you have the paperback or hardback version then type this link into your browser:

https://www.subscribepage.com/author_simon_northouse_subscribe

Follow on Facebook:

https://www.facebook.com/simonnorthouse

Contents

Chapter 1

Start Me Up

Hello, let me introduce myself. My name is Will Harding and I am the singer/songwriter from that famous nineties British rock-and-roll outfit, the "Shooting Tsars". Some of you will have never heard of me or my band; others may have a fuzzy recollection and some melodies skulking away in the recesses of your mind. And of course, all the rest will let out a collective yell of, 'Hail ye, hail ye, Will Harding, singer/songwriter of that brilliant nineties, rock-and-roll band, the Shooting Tsars, huzzah, huzzah!' To those three, I thank you.

I was prompted to put together this diary by a close associate who said Tour Diaries were a great way to give the true fan a "warts and all", "day in the life", "fly on the wall" rockumentary on what it's like to tour the country as part of a rock 'n' roll reunion tour—(don't worry if you think that's a lot of clichés in one paragraph, hold on to your hats, fasten your seatbelts, batten down the hatches, take a deep breath, bath the horse and pickle the radishes—because you ain't see nothing yet good Sir, and Madam).

Now, where was I... I've lost my train of thought, ah, yes, tour diaries. As I was saying, what you will get is a bird's-eye view of life on the road from my perspective. The highs, the lows, the drugs, the sex (actually, there'll be no sex as my mother will read this book, so use your imagination), the music, the characters and the adulation. It's all here in an unabridged, unsanitised, unedited (as you've probably noticed) and unashamed, literary masterpiece.

I'd like to use the words "seminal", "eclectic", and "halcyon" for no other reason than I can. As some of you will be aware, anything written about contemporary music must use these three words at least once to pass the "wank-word" validation test—and I think I have been validated with flying colours.

While I'm at it, I will also throw in "tortured genius", "before his time", "musical colossus" and "discombobulated". The only reason I listed the word "discombobulated", is that it is one of my favourite words—well, each to their own, eh?

I wrote this foreword post-tour, so for me, it is all over—but for you, it is the beginning.

So, without further ado, fasten your seatbelts, hold on to your... hang on, I've already done that. Okay, without further ado, let the tour begin!

Yours,

Will Harding (singer, songwriter, rhythm guitar and seminal, musical colossus.)

Chapter 2

Day 1 – London

I write this as I am sitting on my bed in my hotel room. It is day one of the tour, as you may have deduced from the large, bold heading above. There's one hour to go before we are all due on the tour bus.

I have a cracking hangover thanks to my lack of willpower. I promise, right here, right now, that I am going to curb my drinking. There's work to be done, reputations to be upheld, and new fans to be won over. This tour is not an excuse to overindulge. The odd celebratory drink here and there is fine, but moderation is the key.

Today we head south from London to Southampton, where we will board the ferry to Cowes. We are due to play the Isle of Wight Festival tomorrow, and my nerves are already tingling in anticipation. It is well over a decade ago since The Shooting Tsars last played live together and although we've been rehearsing solidly, playing in front of a "live" audience is a different kettle of turnips.

Chas (our tour manager) took the entire entourage out for a meal last night, which, including all the artists, the road crew, and security, made a grand total of twenty-six people. Being a tight arsed Cockney bullshitter, I assumed that he'd split the bill, but much to my surprise he paid for it all himself. (*Note to self: reword the above sentence before going to press because you know what a litigious little prick Chas can be*). We finished up at the restaurant by about 10 pm, and Chas insisted we all return to our hotel rooms to get an early night. There was much consternation, but we all reluctantly agreed. Once Chas had departed to his room, everyone reconnoitred in the hotel bar, where we proceeded to get slaughtered. We told the barman to chalk it up to Chas's tab. I crawled into bed at 3 am.

11 am: We are all safely ensconced on the tour bus. I've got to say that Chas has done us proud. It's a state-of-the-art sleeper with bunks, kitchen, toilet, TV, video game consoles and brilliant speakers—this is the way to travel.

There is much excitement and banter amongst the bands until Chas arrives on the scene. He stands at the front of the coach with microphone in hand and doesn't look too pleased. He gets our attention and then reprimands us for ten minutes. The bar bill from the hotel was over eight hundred pounds. He calms down and introduces us to our coach driver, Ivan. He tells us that Ivan is as much a part of this tour as anyone and to treat him with respect. Ivan takes the microphone and in broken English, he explains he is a Croatian migrant and has been driving coaches for two years, although this is his first rock-and-roll tour. He is thrilled to be here. We all cheer. Unfortunately for Ivan, before he has even left London, he has knocked a cyclist off his bike, reversed into a black cab, and broken his wing mirror in a bingle with a traffic light. He is promptly re-named Ivan the Terrible.

Someone put U2 on the CD player, which sent Geordie into a rage (they're not his favourite band). He ejected the CD, then launched it out of a window like a Frisbee. We were stationary in the London traffic at the time and the missile hit a passing police officer in the neck, something he didn't take too kindly to. He indicated to Ivan to pull over and entered the coach. Turns out he's a big U2 fan, much to Geordie's chagrin. He gave us all a lecture on the dangers of throwing objects from a vehicle, then let us go on our way. Why do I feel like I'm on a school excursion?

Everything eventually calms down until Chas spots the T-shirt that Geordie is wearing. It's a montage of all the bands with a motif on the front that reads "We thought you were dead Tour". On the reverse, it says "So did I!" Everyone bar Chas found it amusing. Chas tells Geordie to remove the T-shirt to which he receives a few sharp expletives. Chas knows better than to pursue the matter and returns to his seat. However, I can guarantee that Geordie will now sport that T-shirt for the entire tour—unwashed!

Last night in the restaurant, Flaky went around the table and gathered everybody's birth dates. He has been busy plotting an astrological chart for the tour. He goes to the front of the coach and expounds on his predictions. Initially, there was a hush of excitement as he began his first reading. It could have been an entertaining half-hour, but it soon became clear that his verbose, long-winded style and use of non-words made the whole thing a crushing bore. An example, from memory, went something like this;

'June is the lucky month with two full moons, a retrograde in Jupiter, and the exposition of Mars to the east. Geordie, this is your time to transmute your negative energy and plan strategically to manifest benign best practices for the ensuing passage of time, blah—blah—blah.' What in all that's holy, did that even mean? By the time he'd got to the sixth person on his list, everyone bar Divina had switched off. I wish I could switch him off. In what felt like an hour, but was only twenty minutes, he finally gave his prediction for the next forty-eight hours for the tour as a collective.

'Therefore, my chart confidently predicts the Isle of Wight Festival will be a resounding success for every one of our little tribe of musical warriors. Not only that, but the skies will be blue, the Sun will shine and there will be peace, love and understanding in the air.' Complete quackery!

Chapter 3

Day 2 – Isle Of Wight

I awoke with a cracking hangover and felt extremely dehydrated.

Not long after Flaky's astrological predictions of blue sky, peace, love and understanding etc, the heavens opened up, and we were thrown into the jaws of a snarling storm. There was also a small fracas between Effy and Connie.

By the time we made it to the ferry at Southampton, there was talk of closing the crossing down for the day because of the severe weather and dangerously high seas. Luckily, or unluckily, they made one last trip across the Solent. I have never witnessed such violent seas, as the ferry was tossed about like a cork in a washing machine. On many occasions, I prepared to meet my maker. Geordie had got so pissed on the coach that he slept through the whole voyage. Robbo found a little alcove and chain-smoked reefers, seemingly oblivious to the vindictive tempest that raged war outside. The only light relief I got was witnessing Flaky go from a slight wan colour, to pale yellow to a violent green. I have never seen anyone throw up as much as he did. His stomach must be like the inside of the TARDIS.

After two hours, we finally docked in Cowes and disembarked on the Isle of Shite.

Chapter 4

Day 3 – Isle Of Wight

The Festival of Light was played under dark foreboding skies that continually ejected their nebulous load upon the poor wretched souls who had erroneously turned up for fun and entertainment. Divina was first up and became lost on the enormous stage. Poor girl, at least when you're in a group you can always blame the drummer when it goes pear-shaped, but when you're solo, there's nowhere to hide.

We arrived on stage only five minutes late. Chas nearly had a heart attack. It was a lacklustre performance by the Tsars, mainly because the stick man kept breaking off to throw up at the side of the stage. Not a pretty sight for anyone and it wreaked havoc with the tempo of our songs.

I now know what the "sound of one hand clapping" sounds like. This was the noise we left the stage to. Geordie's a bit of a perfectionist when it comes to performing live, and I thought he'd be in a foul mood when we got offstage, but he was quite calm by his own standards. He first sculled a half bottle of whisky, then ripped the door off the trailer and threw it at Flaky. He picked up a bass drum pedal and marched outside. When I asked him what he intended to do with the pedal, he replied he was going to find Chas and shove it into an orifice that was clearly never designed to accommodate such an object. I swear he's mellowing.

As average as we were, there was worse to come. The Green Circles were next on and would have set the house alight, literally, if it hadn't been for a fortuitous shower that put out their improvised pyrotechnics. The penny should have dropped when I saw lead singer—Connie, and bass player—Paddy, sticking four large air bombs down a piece of PVC water pipe before they went onstage. Chas was not amused with their shenanigans, but you know what these Scousers are like, they're always up to something.

Next up were the Stoned Crows. What can one say? Brilliant, fantastic, awesome, inspiring, sublime and stirring! That's exactly right—these are all words one cannot say when describing the Stoned Crows. The day God gave out musical ability, the Crows must have slept in.

Lead singer of the Crows, Effy looked a complete twat in his tight leather pants and pink pirate shirt—for God's sake man, it's not 1984! Effy's lame pants were only matched by the musical equivalent of watching paint dry. Mediocrity, amateurish, hackneyed—and these are their good points. The only plus side of their performance was that it lifted Geordie's spirits as he sat in the wings, chortling away to himself. I don't think I've mentioned the fact that Geordie and Effy don't get along too well.

Chapter 5

The Rogues Gallery

W hat's in a name? Well letters, unless you're R2D2 and then you'd also have a couple of numbers. And of course, there are those weird and scary individuals who use special characters as their name—for example ~#@? Which translates to, "tilde hash-tag at question mark", which I think has quite a ring to it. Anyway, I digress, back to the names.

I deem it appropriate and enlightening to introduce you to a handful of characters before I go any further. They are the main protagonists in my ensuing nightmare... I mean reunion tour. To give you a flavour of their innate traits, foibles and preferred proclivities, I have put pen to paper to give a synopsis of each one. Some may call it character assassination, but I think that is a little harsh; I prefer the phrase "character assignation".

Myself: As you know, (if you bothered to read the foreword), my name is Will Harding, singer/songwriter and founding member of the seminal, eclectic, rock 'n' roll band from the early nineties (halcyon days) The Shooting Tsars. Some of you may read that as Shooting Tasers—well, if you are, you are clearly insane and I suggest you discard this diary in favour of reading matter more in line with your mental capabilities, such as the back of a cornflake packet. It is Tsars, that's right—TSARS. It is not a misspelling of Tasers or Stars—it is not a typo or a clue to a cryptic crossword!

The "Oxbridge, English Upper-Class Twit, Ruling Elite, Dictionary For Word Snobs" describes the word thus; "an emperor of Russia before the ghastly revolution of 1917, when times were a lot better and people knew their station". In other words, a monarch, a king, a ruler. You can spell it Tsar or Tzar or for those with a peculiar bent for obfuscation, Czar. Having read that back, I fear I may have fallen foul of obfuscation myself, due to my use of the word, "obfuscation", but I'll give myself the benefit of the doubt—just this once.

Six months ago I was living a peaceful and reclusive existence in the bosom of my beloved Yorkshire Dales; just me and my dog—Caesar. I'm a working-class kid from Leeds who made good, one lucky break. A decade has passed since the untimely demise of the Shooting Tsars and I had embraced anonymity, peace and tranquillity with open legs. However, a near-death experience, an unexpected and unwelcome telephone call and a cold-caller selling incontinence pads made me re-evaluate my life. And, to cut a long and tedious story short... here I am on the cusp of a British reunion tour with my bandmates and three other artists from the halcyon days of the nineties.

Call it fate, call it madness, call it "greedy old buggers trying to get a second bite of the cherry"—it is what it is—"The Resurrection Tour". But enough of me—onto my fellow bandmates and other malcontents.

Allan "Geordie" Kincaid: The Shooting Tsars bass player extraordinaire, musical colossus, tortured artist, a man before his time and a man past his prime and a royal pain in the rectoleum. As my dear old Gran used to say, "if you can't say anything good about a person, then don't, just slag the twats off!" She had a way with words, my Gran—God bless her.

To be fair, I'll list his bad points first: unnaturally aggressive, argumentative, combative, violent, sarcastic, negative, belligerent, bellicose, opinionated, delusional, unreasonable, dishevelled, uncleanly, slovenly, lazy, indolent, rude, obnoxious, disgusting, and unnaturally, and annoyingly punctual. Having said that, it's only fair I list his good points:

So, having cleared that up, who and what is Geordie? He is six and a half foot Scottish ogre of demonic appearance. He is a Glaswegian born thug with a hard exterior and a soft centre. Geordie looks like a composite of Mick Fleetwood and Arthur Brown of "I am the God of Hell Fire" fame. Scary, right? Wherever Geordie is, there is rancour, discontent, agitation and—entertainment.

Forgive me, I seem to have skipped his good points. Okay, he is a musical genius, I'll give him that. He can turn my rough demos into masterpieces. He can play many instruments; he can concoct three-piece harmonies within minutes, he can instruct, cajole and encourage... but only when it comes to music. It's a gift and one to behold. If truth be known, I should really have given him a fifty-fifty songwriting credit on all of my songs. But then again, did Michelangelo give credit to the guy who built the scaffold for him to paint the Sistine Chapel? I think not!

Gordon Robinson AKA Robbo: The Shooting Tsars lead guitarist, and a bloody good one at that. Robbo is "daddy cool" or at least it appears that way, due to the fact he is stoned out of his box for most of the day... and night. It gives him a cool, laid-back appearance of peace, love and understanding. On the whole, he is a pleasure to be around, mainly because he doesn't disagree with me and is generally "yeah, cool man" about anything I say or do. Robbo is married, childless, and went to Strangegate Comprehensive School in Sheffield where his greatest achievement was winning the sausage raffle in 1978.

John " Flaky" Steele: Flaky is our wonderful drummer but doesn't look or act like a drummer. He looks more like an accountant and acts like Mother Teresa. Alas, Flaky has found God (not sure where), astrology, yoga, running and healthy living—oh, and he doesn't drink alcohol. In the "real" world his sensible grown-up attitude would be admirable—but, he's not in the real world—he's in the rock 'n' roll world where words like moderation, healthy, sleep, and exercise are not only frowned upon but are actively discouraged.

If Flaky has one ounce of sense in him, he'll keep his gob shut and keep a low profile for the entire tour. I love the guy, but he can be a regal pain in the analaseum.

Chas Dupont: I must choose my words carefully when portraying old Chas because he can be a tad litigious. Chas was our manager back in the nineties—then we sacked him—and he took us to court and won. There is history between us... unpleasant history.

Chas is the promoter and tour manager of the Resurrection Tour. In fact, the whole thing is his baby; he put it all together by himself and has put up a not inconsiderable amount of money to do so—or so he says.

Some may say Chas is a Cockney rip-off merchant who would sell his own mother for a Rolex and a bag of chips. Others may accuse Chas of being a duplicitous weasel, a conniving, manipulative, cockney git, never to be trusted. Of course, these are not my words. I would never publicly say anything of the sort.

"So why are you back on tour with him?" I can hear you screaming at the page. Well, the passage of time has mellowed us all and I look back on our halcyon days with bittersweet fondness. We felt it was time to get back up on stage and give the kids what they want; let's call it unfinished business. The poet must write, the sculptor must sculpt, the wandering minstrel must minstrelise and the musician must make music—that, my friend, is the reason. Plus the two hundred grand we each collect for passing go.

We are not alone on this reunion tour. The other acts are:

The Green Circles: Four lovable rogues from Liverpool who were almost as good as we were back in the day. Formed from the ashes of the Madchester scene, the Circles have the best frontman in the game, the diminutive showman and raconteur, Connie.

The Stoned Crows: Not sure where the Crows emanated from because they all have those classless, student type accents which indicate they all had a rather easy and affluent upbringing—not that I hold it against them. I could try to describe their music, but I won't as it makes nauseous to do so.

Divina: The redoubtable, magnificent, Amazonian Goddess. Well, she's not actually Amazonian, she's originally from Birmingham but let's not split hairs. She is a one-man show, but female. Her timeless, dance-inspired songs are still as vibrant and fresh today as they were a decade ago.

And that is the main cast, but there are many supporting actors in this play and you will get to know them as the diary progresses.

Chapter 6

Success!

from the cradle to the rave...

THE SHOOTING TSARS

O ur first album shocked everyone, including ourselves, by hitting the top of the album charts in the UK in its first week of release. It also went to the top spot in France, Germany, Japan, Australia, and Canada. Most surprising of all was the number one position we snared in Madagascar where it knocked "The Sound Of Music Soundtrack" off its pedestal—a pedestal it had been stuck to for over thirty years—the hills were alive with the sound of the Tsars on that day!

To date, it is still the biggest selling album of all time in Madagascar—chalking up a whopping forty-seven album sales—not including the two that were returned!

Chapter 7

Day 4 – Brighton

C has looked a worried man as we all boarded the ferry this morning, but not as worried as a verdant looking Flaky. I have a cracking hangover and plan to give myself an alcohol-free day.

We are on our way to Brighton now. Mood is still good on the coach, despite the festival nightmare. Geordie seems to have entered into a friendly rivalry with Connie from the Circles as to who can pull off the most outlandish behaviour—I hope it doesn't get out of hand.

⟫⟫ ⟪⟪

A much better performance by all except the Crows, who for some unexplained reason headlined again! Flaky is nearly back to normal (unfortunately) and incessant nagging has resumed. Tension is growing between Geordie and Effy, and Geordie and Flaky, and Connie and Effy, and Effy and Chas, and... well, you get the picture.

Had a pleasant chat with Divina after her performance. The woman is a goddess. Ticket sales were poor. Chas was hoping for four thousand, but lucky if he got fifteen hundred through the door. Ah well, at least we're still getting paid. Did the usual mindless interviews.

Chapter 8

Day 5 – Bristol

I 'm feeling a little delicate today as we head west to Bristol. I once again foolishly over-imbibed, but I've made myself a promise to only drink in moderation after the gig tonight.

The mood on the bus is a little strained this morning. The Circles and the Tsars all agree on one thing—the Stoned Crows should not be headlining! When we mentioned this "fact" to the Crows, it did not go down well. Chas has agreed to rotate the bands tonight.

Sat at the back of the coach with Divina for a while and discussed Byron, Keats and Shelley. Very stimulating. Then had a chat with Robbo who told me about his bunions, haemorrhoids and dicky knee... slightly less stimulating.

Typically, there's sixteen of us on the coach each day, which includes the bands, and Chas, and Ivan. But this number can swell to twenty or more. For the last couple of days, we've had a film crew making a "rockumentary" about the Resurrection Tour. The crew comprises a cameraman, sound engineer, producer and interviewer. There are usually a couple of hacks and accompanying photographers from the weekly music rags that tag along for two or three days, garnering interviews, photos and drinking the free beer and wine that is on offer.

It can often be a difficult situation when you stick so many personalities together in a confined space. Remember, present company excepted, these people own colossal egos! A lot of them are vying to be top dog and their tipping point is a lot lower than your normal, socially, well-adjusted person.

The upside is the road crew are not on the coach. One must be thankful for small mercies! They have their own transport arrangements and typically set off well before our coach departs. Now don't get me wrong, I love our road crew; they are a great bunch of guys if you can handle the smell. I always make a point of chatting with them before and after the gig to show my appreciation. Well, it's not really a chat. They grunt something and I try to decipher what it is they are saying. It's a bit like charades, but not as much fun.

On tour friction is inevitable and there have been many "bust-ups" already. Only this morning there was a mass brawl between the lads from the Green Circles and the wankers from the Stoned Crows. At first, I assumed it was a clash of ego and personality. Maybe someone made the front page of the music papers and someone else didn't. Or it could be an argument about who is headlining at the next show. As I said, there are fragile egos at play. As it turned out, the ruckus started because Connie helped himself to the last pot-noodle which Effy had been eying up.

I try my best to keep out of the petty squabbles and back-biting. I do this by following my golden rule I developed over fifteen years ago when I first began touring. It has stood me in good stead ever since. It is the "T" word—tolerance.

It's a simple philosophy but is amazingly effective. Whatever gripes people have, whatever ridiculous things they say or do, I accept them for who they are, good, bad, or in the Stoned Crows case, indifferent. It's about putting away resentment, jealousy, and even hatred. Tolerance is the oil that... well, oils the wheels. It's really not that hard to do —as Robbo would say, "Peace, love and understanding."

***

I swear to God, if Flaky lectures me one more time about my drinking, smoking or unhealthy diet, I'm going to rip his beaky faced head from his scrawny shoulders!

Chapter 9

The Difficult Second Album

So much for the so-called "difficult" second album. Wasn't difficult at all! Write songs, rehearse, then record. Hey punk – keep it simple! We finished the album in seven days. It takes the bands of today that amount of time to find the right snare sound!

The truth of the matter is, if you knew my bandmates, you'd want to spend as little time in their company as possible.

For our last album "Buddha's Playground", we'd taken to recording separately. I'd record my parts in the morning, Geordie would record in the afternoon, and Robbo would record at night. As for Flaky, we recorded his drums, long-distance, via the telephone speakerphone. Got to admit, we all got on fine.

Chapter 10

Day 6 – Stonehenge

T oday is a free day and last night I arranged with Divina to hire a car and visit Stonehenge. The woman is a mine of information and extremely knowledgeable about many things. Unfortunately, some of the other band members caught wind of our historical sojourn and invited themselves along for the ride. Geordie, Robbo and Connie thought it would be a great hoot. Divina had to drive the outward journey as I feared I was still "over-the-limit" and I'm pretty certain the other three were as well.

There are many theories about Stonehenge, not just how the stones got there, but also what their purpose was. Some suggest it is an ancient Druid burial site or the terminus for a funeral procession. Others link it to the stars, planets and satellites—an astrological calendar. And then there are a few, well, two actually, who insist it was an ancient football ground; the pillars were goal posts, the lintel a crossbar. And lastly, there's the stoner— who says it is a landing strip for alien spaceships and why can't we all see it, maaan!

I have my own theory. I believe Stonehenge is the earliest incarnation of local town planning. Flogoff, a local town planner, fresh-faced from Druid University, decided the old wooden village that had served its inhabitants extremely well for over a millennium, should be bulldozed and replaced with a high-rise, open plan living experience, with exquisite views to die for and thermal generated uploads. I can imagine the local inhabitants would have been very busy sending "stiff" slates to the local newspaper.

'Why does council persist in pushing this half-baked idea of high rise living on to the good folk of Henge!'

'It appears local council cannot find the funds to repair my pig trough but can pour thousands of Grunts into the building of what I can only describe as a carbuncle to the eye!'

'Town Planner Flogoff may have a fancy-dancy education but let me assure him—if he thinks stone is the next great leap forward in architectural design, he has another think coming!'

Of course, as with all town planning, it ended up being an expensive folly, funded by the weary taxpayer. The dodgy contractor the council employed didn't install a damp proof course, so the building was full of mould. The windows didn't fit because they hadn't yet invented glass. The lifts continually broke down. Gangs of disaffected youths began loitering around the front doors, harassing the elderly and people with excessive nasal hair. The final straw came when persons unknown, began urinating in the stairwell, at which point the site was abandoned and a new timber village, "Woodhenge" was built a few miles down the road.

For his clear ineptitude, town planner Flogoff would have been elected as Lord Mayor of Henge. A few years later he entered Druidic politics, possibly as Grand Master of Proctology. His untimely death, aged 27, by being internally ruptured by a Clydesdale Horse, would have come as a great loss to the community.

Well... it's only a theory.

Chapter 11

Day 7 – London

The music press and newspaper journalists play a crucial role in the success of a tour. It is essential we get positive reviews early on to help build momentum and create a buzz. Enough excellent reviews and things snowball and take on a life of their own. On the other hand, bad reviews can sound the death knell for even the most well-organised tour. Of course, there's only a finite number of reporters and photographers to go around, and every band currently touring the country will harangue the papers to send a journalist and photographer to cover their concert. This creates a bit of a dilemma, but I have to hand it to Chas, he is the master when it comes to getting publicity.

First of all, he rings the editor of the music press and tabloids and offers twenty free tickets, which the editor can distribute to whomever. If this doesn't work, he informs them there will be free food and drink on offer for reporter and photographer alike. This usually brings forth a positive response. But there are always a stubborn few who refuse these incentives, stating the paper's ethical integrity would be compromised by such sweeteners. It is completely up to the editor to decide which concerts they review and which bands they feature on their front cover. It is the basis of the free press and an integral part of democracy. In these rare instances of someone occupying the moral high ground, Chas has no alternative but to offer them five grams of top-notch cocaine upon arrival at the gig. Needless to say, it has never failed yet.

Another important weapon in Chas's promotional arsenal is to invite as many "A" list celebrities as possible. These can include the latest film or TV star, the biggest comedians or sports personalities. He skips right past the free tickets, food and drink as it's a given with the "A" listers. Instead, he jumps straight to the coke. He knows they will be followed by the paparazzi, and a few days later there will be photos in all the gossip magazines of some VIP entering our gig with grace, dignity and charisma. Four hours later they will be leaving the gig, off their tits, hair all over the place, lipstick smeared across their face and stockings dangling from their necks... and that's just the men!

Of course, it's not always possible to get as many "A" list celebrities as one would like. Sometimes he has to invite some "B" listers to make up the numbers. "B" listers are typically people who used to be famous but now have a serious drug and alcohol problem. These types can actually be a very effective promotional weapon because by the time they are forcibly ejected from the gig by security, they are ready for a good punch-up with the awaiting paparazzi. It all makes for another rush of free publicity. Chas calls it "traction".

Tonight was "blaggers" night, and it was a resounding success. I thought Chas had made a mistake by letting the Stoned Crows headline, but by the time they took to the stage, anybody who was anybody was upstairs in the private bar getting their rocks off.

Chapter 12

Day 8 – London

H ell of a hangover this morning, so I scored some whizz off Robbo and instantly felt better.

Flaky and Geordie had a massive bust-up this morning, which I thought was going to result in Flaky taking an impromptu flying lesson through the hotel window. Considering we are on the twenty-fifth floor, it may have proved less than desirable.

You may wonder what caused the argument. Drugs, religion, politics, the breakdown of the middle-east peace talks? No, it was a dispute as to whether Zebedee from the Magic Roundabout is a radish or a carrot. Flaky insisted the old jack-in-the-box is a radish while Geordie argued in favour of a carrot. They are both delusional—Zebedee was undoubtedly a tomato!

Chapter 13

Day 9 – Birmingham

When I woke up this morning, it took me a good ten minutes to recall which city I was in and what day it was. Finally, my memory returned, and I realised it was Wednesday and we had the day off, which cheered me up no end. Unfortunately, I also recalled where I was and my cheerfulness duly evaporated. Birmingham—England's second city—always the bridesmaid and never the bride, and my God, what an ugly bridesmaid she is.

The band had breakfast together, and it was decided we should give Birmingham a chance and do a bit of sightseeing, and sample the pleasures it had on offer. We set off at 10 am from the hotel with a bounce in our step and a twinkle in our eye.

Thirty minutes later we were all back at the hotel twiddling our thumbs, deciding what we could do for the rest of the day. Flaky headed for a swim, and Robbo went back to bed. I was sitting in my room with Geordie, I, reading a newspaper while Geordie watched Playschool. There was a knock on the door, and in walks Chas.

'Hey Will, have you got anything on for the next hour or so?' he asked.

'Well, I've got a pair of jeans on, a polo shirt and a pair of Adidas trainers—why? Do you want me to get naked? Is there something you need to tell me?' He smiled at me like a weary parent with an irksome child.

'Listen, I have a live online chat set up with Kick Music Magazine and I need someone responsible to answer fan questions. It's a bit of free promotion. Are you up for it?'

'I suppose so. I'm not technically minded when it comes to computers and the internet though.'

'You don't need to be. I'll bring my laptop in here and set it all up for you. All you need to do is sit at the laptop, fans will type questions and you answer them—it's simple. There's a moderator from Kick who will be overseeing things so you don't get any personal questions or abusive comments.'

The idea didn't thrill me, but at least it would chew up a good hour of the moribund day. I got myself a strong coffee, made myself comfortable in front of the laptop and the "Live Chat" began.

"Hello Will, I've been a long-time fan of the Tsars and am really excited you and the boys are back together. Why were you away for ten years?" Peter Barrowclough – Cleveland.

"Hey Peter, thanks for your support over the years. Good question, and not entirely sure how to answer it. I suppose life sometimes happens and before you know it, a decade has passed. We definitely needed a break from each other, and the record business, after our disastrous court case, but I never envisaged it would last this long. Enjoy it while it lasts! Ha Ha!" Will Harding – The Shooting Tsars.

"Hi Will, have you got any new material on the horizon, maybe a new album?" Steve – Bournemouth.

"Hello Steve, I've got a pile of songs in a suitcase stuck under my bed. This tour is solely about the old songs, though. Give everyone a chance to reminisce. As for doing a new album – well, we'll have to wait and see how the tour goes, and how we all feel about being back together again." Will Harding – The Shooting Tsars.

'Morning Will, there's been a persistent rumour amongst Tsarists that there is a long-lost album called "Bloom". Some even claim to have a demo tape of it (although I have never actually heard it). Are the rumours true?" Alice Davenport – Whitby.

"And good morning to you, Alice. Again, not sure how to answer this one. Maybe there once was a tape called "Bloom" – or maybe there wasn't. But I can assure you of one thing – if there was – then it certainly does not exist today – that's if it ever existed – which it may not have. Anyone who says they have a demo of it is an attention seeking reprobate or clinically insane." Will Harding – The Shooting Tsars.

And so it progressed for a good twenty minutes. I needed to take a leak, and I was also pining for a cigarette, so I asked Geordie to take over my duties for a few minutes. He reluctantly agreed. I visited the bathroom, then snuck outside and had a smoke before returning to my room. When I entered, I was surprised to see Geordie sitting back in front of the TV watching an old black and white film.

'What are you doing?' I enquired.

'Watching a film, what does it look like,' he replied nonchalantly.

'What's happened to the live chat?'

'It's finished.' I checked my watch. The live chat had barely been going thirty minutes, and I could swear Chas had said it would last for an hour or more. Before I could make any further enquiries, there was a loud rap on the door, followed by Chas's angry voice.

'Jesus H Christ, Will! What do you think you're playing at?' I opened the door as a red-faced Chas burst in. 'I've had the editor of Kick on the phone tearing strips off me!' I was bemused, to say the least.

'I'm not sure what you're on about, Chas. What's the problem?'

'The problem,' he blustered, 'the problem is the moderator has closed the chat down!'

'Why? Did someone leave an abusive comment or something?'

'Yes! You!' I threw a glance at Geordie, who was resolutely staring directly at the TV. I checked the laptop and scrolled back to where I'd left off and where Geordie had taken over. It all started off innocuously enough, but then quickly descended into abuse, threat and counter-threat.

"So, the Shooting Tsars are back together! The question is... why? You were crap the first time around and ten years off the treadmill will not have changed that indelible fact. Pack up and go home, you pot-bellied, grey-haired, old tosspot, has-beens!" Greaserr – The Moon.

"Hello Greaser1, you f**king moron. Come down to the Clinton Hotel in Birmingham City Centre and I'll show you who is a has-been! You hard-boiled, sack of scrotum sweat!" Will Harding – The Shooting Tsars.

"I agree with Greaser1 – you turd suckers are only back for the money. So much for music, truth and integrity, eh? They all succumb in the end. Sad day for music. You've now sullied your once legendary status and are just another bunch of grasping, spoilt rock stars." Dave Getty – Leeds.

"Dear Dave, why don't you crawl back into the septic tank that is your life and do something worthwhile for the benefit of society – like cut your f**king head-off!" Will Harding - The Shooting Tsars.

"What a wanker, there's no need for that!" Jerry K – London

"Agree, total wanker – 100%! Another arrogant, cosseted pop star who can't take even the mildest of criticisms." H – Cardiff.

'What a cock-smoking piece of arrogant northern scum!!!!!'

Pauly – Dartford

"Yeah, and why don't you bunch of losers go give yourselves a battery acid enema? You're all full of shit! Get f**ked!" Will Harding - The Shooting Tsars.

"This online chat has now been shut down due to inappropriate language and physical threats and bullying. It will not be re-opened." The Moderator – Kick Magazine.

Chapter 14

Day 10 – Cardiff

I'm writing this as I'm sitting on the bus, heading southwest into the land of leeks and peaks. Tonight's gig will be like placing a pea on a drum. The venue usually holds forty thousand hairy arsed Welshmen, if we get one-tenth of that we'll be lucky. Chas is not on the bus today. He had business to take care of in London and will see us tomorrow for our London gig.

Connie and Geordie procured a cricket bat and a bag full of tennis balls from somewhere and began a game of coach cricket. If you hit a window it's four, if you get it out of the window it's six and if you hit anyone on the back of the head, you're out. Flaky joined in and delivered a lame underarm ball to Connie who crunched a powerful straight drive back down the coach. The ball ricocheted off the driver's window at an alarming rate and hit poor old Ivan squarely in the eye. The coach veered violently across two lanes of the motorway before Ivan regained control of the vehicle. We had to stop at the nearest services and purchase ice to ease the swelling. Ivan the terrible has now been renamed one-eyed Ivan.

Everyone seems in good humour, (apart from Ivan). Even the Stoned Crows look chilled out after their harrowing start to the tour.

Chapter 15

What Goes Up, Must Come Down

O ur last officially released album and this time we broke into the top ten in the USA. Making it in the States is the Holy Grail of all bands because of the size of the market. The mega-big time was waiting for us around the corner—a corner where we lost control, crashed through the safety barrier and flew over a cliff.

Chapter 16

Day 11 – London

F eel like death warmed up—cracking hangover.

The mood on the coach is subdued. Geordie and Connie both went out for an Indian last night, trying to outdo each other as to who could handle the hottest curry. The competition was a draw when they both finished two helpings of prawn Vindaloo and six onion bhajis. However, the chemical toilet took a hammering this morning and the whole coach has become embalmed in a violent miasma. I'm not sure how much more of this I can take.

⇌⇌⇌ ⇋⇋⇋

Things go from bad to worse. When we arrived at the hotel, there'd been a mixup with the room allocations and it transpires we cannot get a single room each and have to share a double. This poses a dilemma for me. If I've got to share a room with one of my bandmates, I'd obviously pick Robbo. He's easy-going and laid back. Plus, the constant chain-smoking of reefers creates a dense hemp smog, which relaxes me and helps me sleep. But, if I choose Robbo, that would leave Geordie and Flaky to room together, which is akin to tucking up a chicken and a fox together for the night. Therefore, my options are either Flaky or Geordie. I tried weighing up the pros and cons of both worst-case scenarios but could only come up with a long list of cons. Geordie farts, coughs, snores and sleeps with the window open. Flaky is early to bed, early to rise, complains about everything and would no doubt lecture me long into the night. These are the behind-the-scenes quandaries the average Joe Blow doesn't see or understand. I might ask Divina if I can room with her, we could top and tail so to ensure there're no shenanigans!

Chapter 17

Unequivocally Quashing The Rumour

This album never existed. But we did have an idea for the cover. That's God's honest truth!

There's an urban legend which has grown up around our last-last album "Bloom". It has become almost mythical. Well, I'm here to put the record straight once and for all. I'll word it as simply and logically as I can, so no one can be left in any doubt about the truth.

We intended to record Bloom but our record company slapped an injunction on us which meant we could not rehearse, record or play live together until the dispute was resolved.

I can categorically say, unequivocally, Bloom does not exist and if it ever did exist (which it didn't), then it doesn't now or at least it wouldn't have if we'd ever recorded it, which we didn't, therefore it is... or is not... something that was... or maybe wasn't.

I hope this has clarified everything and now it's time to put the matter to bed.

(Note to self: reword the above before going to press. It's utter drivel! I've fallen foul of obfuscation yet again. You're a complete disgrace, Harding!)

Chapter 18

Day 12 – Leeds

What a day! The Tsars were in charge of publicity and we were given a hire car to make our way to Leeds ahead of the other bands to do some last-minute radio interviews. I had been looking forward to getting off the coach for a while, but the feeling of relief and optimism was short-lived.

For reasons I cannot go into at the moment, we became involved in an imbroglio on the motorway. This resulted in our arrest and a court appearance for two band members, who shall remain nameless (Geordie and Robbo). Luckily, we were released in time to still make it to the gig. This is show business and as they say, "the show must go on!" Plus, there's also a clause in our contract which states if we miss a gig, we forfeit twenty-five percent of our total tour money.

Chapter 19

Day 13 – Manchester

It's 10 am, and I am writing this diary entry relaxing at the back of the coach. We are making our way across the Pennines as we head from Leeds to Manchester for tonight's gig. I have given myself a little "pat-on-the-back" as it is my first morning without a hangover. Now, this may be because I am still pleasantly drunk—but let's not split hairs.

I didn't think yesterday could get any worse after the motorway debacle but how wrong I was. The gig itself had been a resounding success, and we could have sold it out three times over. However, the post-gig celebrations proved to be our downfall. Getting arrested twice in the space of twelve hours must have set some kind of record.

We were released from the police cells four hours ago into a dreary, cold and rainy morning, without, may I add, not even so much as a cup of tea from our boys in blue. I thought the worst was behind me. However, my pessimistic optimism was soon shattered when we all arrived at the hotel bar. Chas awaited us and once he had bought us all double whiskeys and dispensed his white tonic powder, he threw a bunch of newspapers onto the countertop. Tabloid journalism—what would the world be like without it? Well, the obvious answer is; a damn sight better! I can't go into too much detail here as the lawyer who is representing Robbo and Geordie has advised us all to keep shtum. But let me say this, the story has been blown out of all proportion. Facts have been deliberately omitted, and there is a lot of supposition, assumptions and commentary about the incident which are just plain wrong. And this is the story about the motorway incident. I dread to think what tomorrow's headlines will scream when the tabloids find out about the fight we had later on in the evening.

We also made top billing on all the breakfast news channels. One inbred conservative MP actually demanded we apologise to the Royal Family immediately or be thrown into the Tower of London. Considering the Tower has been a tourist attraction for at least a hundred and fifty years, I'm not sure what kind of punishment this would be. Although on reflection, ten minutes in the gift shop may be a fate worse than death.

Chas was delighted with the rush of negative publicity and I believe ticket sales for the remaining concerts have skyrocketed.

Chapter 20

Day 14 – Newcastle

S ure enough, we hit the front pages again. But at least today we garnered some sympathy when it was revealed the fight began because we were standing up to racism. Well, I wasn't actually standing at the time, I was sitting and within a few seconds of the fracas beginning, I was slumping, followed by lying prostrate and barely conscious —but you get my drift. The rush of unwarranted publicity has ensured the rest of the tour has completely sold out. Chas may even break even at this rate.

As we came offstage tonight after our third encore and relaxed backstage, I reflected on the first gig we ever did together as The Shooting Tsars. It was in the mid-nineties, not long after Geordie first joined the group. We had convinced a pub landlord to let us play. It was free entry but if we pulled in more than his usual custom for a Wednesday night, he'd bung us twenty quid. We did a rush of publicity for the gig, which mainly involved driving around in a car and fly posting large A1 sized posters on any spare wall we could find. We even stuck one onto the side of a number 44 bus as it sat idling at a terminus.

The pub had a small stage, two feet off the ground, and featured a tiny dance floor in front of it. At 7:30 pm we took to the stage and launched into our first song. When it ended I said "Thanks, thanks very much" and to this day I'm still not sure why. There was nothing, not a cheer, not a handclap, not even a boo! I stared at the faces as they sat mute in their chairs. The entire crowd stared back at me with open mouths and eyes agape. It was like we were aliens from another solar system that had landed in their pub for a quick pint of beer and a pickled egg. It was the most disconcerting reaction I've ever received.

We all hope for loud applause and cheers; I can get by with a muted response and I can even accept boos and deranged hecklers. But nothing... only the sound of my thumping heart. The crowd reaction so discombobulated us all we did the only thing possible in that situation—we played faster. The faster we played the more furious my guitar playing became. Halfway through the set, I broke a string, and I didn't have a replacement. Next song I bust another string. After each song, I would re-tune my guitar, but it had taken umbrage at being played with only four strings and doggedly refused to keep in tune. Still nothing from the crowd.

We got to our last song, and I said, "Okay, thanks for coming tonight, this is our last song". I was a bit of a raconteur in those days. We blasted through the last tune in record time, as though we had a bus to catch. We ended and there was a five-second pause before the crowd erupted into life. They jumped from their seats and began clapping, cheering and whistling. "Encore! Encore!" they chanted. The band was totally nonplussed, but we obliged and began an encore. At this point, the crowd suddenly remembered what to do, and many of them took to the dancefloor. We played on for another thirty minutes until the landlord called time. Welcome to rock 'n' roll!

Chapter 21

Day 15 – Glasgow

We are on Geordie's home turf, and I've got to say his mood has changed dramatically. He is now argumentative, obnoxious, aggressive and truculent... it's amazing how playing in your hometown can improve one's disposition for the better. He's almost a pleasure to be around.

When on tour, it is imperative to look after your body. Apart from regular exercise (getting out of bed, walking to the coach, lifting bottles of brown liquid), you should never neglect your diet. If you want to survive thirty days on the road, you must fuel your body with nutritious energy. For example, tonight I forewent my usual takeaway curry and opted for a healthier Chinese takeaway meal instead. I always make sure, post-gig, I hydrate myself with five or six bottles of beer followed by a bottle or two of white wine before I even look at the spirits! Beer is ninety-five percent water and white wine is about ten percent water. I believe it is this parsimonious routine that has kept me energised and vital throughout our gruelling regime.

I have even cut back on the cigarettes. There's a lot of downtime when on the road, and it is a trap to alleviate the monotony by continually chain-smoking. Therefore, during daylight hours, I replace cigarettes with cigars. It's absolutely impossible to smoke as many cigars in a day as it is cigarettes—it's too damn expensive. Do you know the cost of a fine Havana these days!

Chapter 22

Cutting Corners

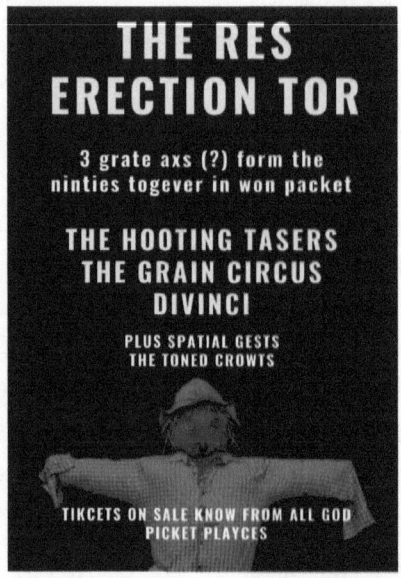

To save money Chas handed the tour poster design over to his nephew, a design student at Liverpool Uni. Chas was unaware the poor lad suffers from dyslexia.

Chas has many faults, one of them being his tendency to cut corners and do things on the "cheap". A prime example is the original tour poster above. Instead of going to a reputable printer and getting the job done correctly, he used his nephew, who is studying fine art at Liverpool University. At the time, Chas didn't know his nephew suffered from dyslexia. Well, he knows now! Ten thousand posters had to be ditched—an expensive lesson!

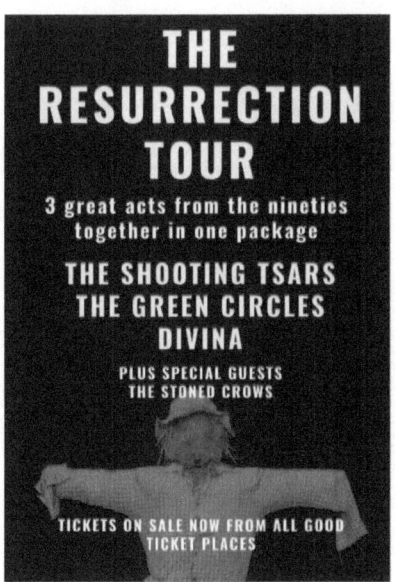

And this is how it was supposed to look. Unfortunately, the Stoned Crows kicked up a stink for being labelled "Special Guests", a euphemism in the music business for "utter shite!". Another ten thousand posters down the clacker!

Chapter 23

Day 16 – Glasgow

W e played two blistering gigs in Glasgow where the crowd went totally insane! Although to be fair, the Glaswegians have an unfair advantage in that department. They certainly love their music in this neck-of-the-woods and show their appreciation. However, one of our entourage received terrible news tonight with the passing of a very close family member and it obviously, and rightly, subdued the celebrations somewhat.

There was also more bad news when some high jinks got out of hand, resulting in both Connie from the Green Circles and Effy from the Stoned Crows being hospitalised. Luckily for Connie, all he suffered was a dislocated shoulder. However, Effy took a bone-crunching blow to the jaw, and it was feared he would not be able to sing again. When he returned some hours later, he delivered the bad news to everyone. Despite a split lip and missing a tooth, his voice was unaffected, and he intended to carry on with the tour. A sad night for everyone on many fronts.

Chapter 24

Day 17 – Sunderland

T oday we are in Sunderland, which I believe is an old Norse word for "shithole". Why the Vikings ever landed here is beyond me, but land they did. Once they'd finished pillaging and checking their Lotto tickets, they installed a puppet king and buggered off—which is exactly what I would like to do now—but alas, I have a gig to do.

Excessive alcohol intake; enough class "A" drugs to make the eyes bleed; unrelenting sex with anything which moves; VIP hotel suites; first-class air travel; stretch limousines; queue-jumping at famous restaurants and nightclubs; people hanging on your every word as though a prophet; adulation, attention, fame and Dom Perignon enemas from a successful and well-trained dominatrix! This is what the average Joe-public-punter thinks the life of a rock 'n' roll star is like. Well, let me put you straight—it's all completely true! But, it's not all beer and skittles. First and foremost, rock 'n' roll is a business. It's like a shoe shop. In the window are the shoes, all shiny and new, but behind the scenes is the cobbler. Blackened thumbs, gnarled lips, leather apron, nails in mouth and porno mags in the toolbox. It's not easy, let me tell you! But there is one thing more important than anything else... the golden rule which must never be broken. It is five letters long and begins with "T" and ends in "T". Got it yet? No, it's not "taunt, trout or twixt". It is "TRUST!" Knock the "T" off trust and what do you get? RUST! (Although technically, you could also get "TRUS" but let's not get bogged down in semantics). Trust is everything, and there is a palpable lack of it between the Tsars and our inglorious tour manager. Enough said!

Chapter 25

Day 18 – Liverpool

I write this as I sit backstage in Liverpool. There is an unusual calmness that pervades the atmosphere. Guitars are being tuned up, cigarettes are smoked and there's a quiet chatter amongst the bands. I can hear the crowd in the distance cheering enthusiastically as Divina goes through her set.

I like Liverpool; I like Liverpudlians. And we all know, the greatest band of all time came from these hallowed streets—yes, The Flock Of Seagulls.

Liverpudlians always manage to laugh. No matter how bad times are or what tragedies strike, there is always humour. I like their spirit and resilience—it sums up the human condition—upwards and onwards, never be beaten, keep on keeping on. The place has character, history and a proud catalogue of truly great music. Yes, Liverpool is my kind of city and Liverpudlians are my kind of people.

This is my last diary entry of the day. I'm back in my hotel room and I'm seething with an incandescent white rage! Some Scouse twat has stolen my prized Gibson ES-335! Never, ever, trust a Scouser! It's the last time I set foot in this hell-hole of a city!

Chapter 26

Day 19 – Sheffield

G ood news! My precious Gibson has been returned unscathed to my loving arms. When the boys from the Green Circles heard about what happened, they assured me they would leave no stone unturned in their endeavours to find my purloined instrument. Coming from Liverpool, they immediately phoned all their contacts and put out the word; the guitar must be returned! This morning there was a gentle knock on my hotel door and you can imagine my joy when I opened it to see a grinning Connie standing there with my guitar. There was a small finder's fee of one thousand pounds which I first had to hand over, but it was a mere trifle compared to the sentimental value the instrument holds for me. Blessed be the Scousers.

For reasons best known to himself, tonight Effy decided to embellish his all in one leather jumpsuit with a sword and scabbard. To say he looked like a total prick would be an understatement. I think he sees himself as an 18th century romantic, a modern-day Lord Byron. Muffled laughter greeted him as he walked on stage, and that was from his own band. My Grandad had an old saying, "the higher a monkey climbs the more it shows its arse" – a bit of a poet my old Pa.

Chapter 27

Day 20 – Wolverhampton

When I awoke this morning, I immediately had a full-on panic attack. I was convinced that during the night I had gone blind. I opened my eyes, but everything was pitch black. I knew it was morning because I had a throbbing hangover and could hear traffic outside the hotel window.

I've heard about people going blind from drinking too much alcohol and convinced myself this had happened to me. I realised there and then how much we take sight for granted. I envisioned my life without being able to see, and it wasn't a pretty sight—if you know what I mean.

How would I get showered and dressed each day? How would I cook food, make a cup of tea, get the top off a bottle of beer? The simplest tasks would take up most of the day. But the most shocking aspect is I'd never be able to watch porn again—what a calamity! Is porn the same without vision? I've certainly watched porn with the sound off, but never the other way around.

Luckily, I regained my sight almost immediately when I realised I'd put on a sleeping mask before retiring to bed, but let me tell you—it was a close call and a chastening one. It has made me more determined than ever to get off the booze for a few days.

Chapter 28

Day Whatever – Somewhere

N ot sure what day it is or where I am or even who I am. This tour must end soon otherwise I will need to donate my brain and liver to medical science as a lesson to humanity.

I thought some mean-spirited bastard was playing a bass drum somewhere in the hotel until I realised it was the blood vessels pounding in my head. I need water, and paracetamol, and ibuprofen—in fact, euthanasia is looking decidedly attractive at the moment.

For some reason, there is the upper torso of a female mannequin in my bed. At least I hope it's a mannequin. I can't see any blood. When I stand up, the floor feels spongy. When I sit down, foreign objects dart across my eyes. If I lie down, the room spins. I am the chief protagonist in Dante's Inferno—next stop, purgatory. Whoever invented alcohol needs disembowelling—slowly. Can barely read this scrawl back and I'm using a keyboard!

Chapter 29

Day 22 – Bournemouth

I t was my turn to do the pre-gig interview with the local radio station. I didn't really see the point as the gig was completely sold out, but it's in the contract, so I must obey. Geordie came along for the ride. I was running late and couldn't find a parking spot. I had the radio on and the presenter kept saying, "With us shortly is the frontman from the Shooting Tsars, Will Harding, so if you have any questions for him, text them through now!" I let Geordie out of the car and told him to hot-foot it to the radio station and explain I would be with them as soon as possible. Five minutes later, I found a space and parked up. I was about to turn the radio off when the presenter made another announcement.

"Hello, listeners! Live in the studio I have Geordie from the Shooting Tsars, remember to send your texts in now if you any questions..." I broke out in a hot sweat and my sphincter involuntary clenched.

I must admit, it was a funny joke if told in the confines of a hotel room or backstage, but, one cannot say those things on a live radio broadcast! I wrote a letter of apology to the presenter and to the management of the radio station. Chas donated a cheque for five thousand pounds to the local Catholic Church, hoping it would assuage the outrage of the nuns. Alas, it still didn't stop rent-a-mob turning up outside the concert hall, shouting slogans and waving placards. "Burn the Satanists", "God will strike thee down", "Ban the Tasers" and my own personal favourite, "Stop cruelty to guinea pigs". I think that particular protestor may have got on the wrong bus. Robbo was going to inform the guy with the "Tasers" placard he had spelt "Tsars" incorrectly, but I advised against it.

No doubt the tabloids will be screaming their feigned outrage in the morning. I can see the headlines now, "Rock Band's Bad Habits Continue", "An Unholy Mess" and "Sick Joke Is Nun Too Funny".

Due to the death threats we received, we thought it wise to hire a car and head straight to London the minute we got off stage. It will be a very long time before we can play Bournemouth again—if ever—so there's always an upside to every situation.

Chapter 30

Day 23 – London

I've already explained how important it is to keep one's body adequately fuelled, hydrated and exercised while touring. But, I forgot to mention another equally important rule. One must keep the brain engaged! The mind must be stimulated on a daily basis to ward off the ravages of dementia and senility. The fact is, life on the road can be extremely boring most of the time. From hotel room to coach, from coach to hotel, from hotel to drug dealer, from drug dealer to brothel, from brothel to sound-check; the whole thing can become mind-numbing. And then there's the added danger of inadvertently talking to the roadies—this sort of interaction can leave the brain in permanent stasis.

I use two methods to keep my grey matter regenerating at an exponential rate.

Firstly, I ponder the questions that have plagued humankind since the dawn of time. Questions the great philosophers have wrestled with over the aeons. Names like Socrates, Plato, Nietzsche, Confucius and Jean Paul Gaultier have all tackled the eternal dilemmas. Who am I? Why am I here? What is my purpose? Did I turn the oven off? And the biggest conundrum of all—why did Geordie only pack two pairs of underpants for an eight-week tour? These questions can keep my mind occupied for at least a few minutes each day.

Secondly, I tackle a cryptic crossword on a daily basis... once my hangover has subsided. You really need to think outside of the square, in front of the box, inside the circle and at forty-five degrees to the hypotenuse to complete a cryptic. Unfortunately, today there was one clue I could not complete no matter how long I spent on it. The clue was thus; "take the last shuttle, lose room while dancing, and turn the water off". I know, I know! You'll all be laughing at my stupidity—it's so blindingly obvious now!

However, it led to a most embarrassing incident during tonight's gig. We'd finished our third song, and the applause and cheering were slowly fading away when the answer came to me in a blinding flash. I unwittingly yelled into the microphone, "BALLCOCK!"

Now, bear in mind, there were over forty thousand people in the audience tonight, plus a film crew, plus "A" and "B" list celebrities, lesser-known royals (of which there are many), my mother, my girlfriend and record company executives. For a few ghastly seconds, the whole arena fell completely silent. They must have wondered whether I had developed the rapid onset of Tourettes. Even my fellow band members, who are more than used to my stranger moments, eyed me with cryptic suspicion. But at least I completed the damn crossword!

Chapter 31

Day 24 – London (again) And The End... Thank God!

T onight is our last gig and before The Stoned Crows went on stage, I gathered everyone's attention backstage and made a little speech in honour of our thankless road crew.

'Thank you, everyone. I'd like to say a little something to the unsung heroes as this tour draws to a close tonight. Now, we, the artists and bands receive all the adulation, the fame, the headlines... and quite rightly so—it is the natural order of things and long may it continue. And Chas, well, he gets all the money (cue laughter). But there is a tireless crew or is it tiresome, which works behind the scenes of every single gig. Yes, I'm talking about security!

No, only joking, it is, of course, our fabulous road crew, without whom, none of this would have been possible.

I'd like to thank Tony, our sound engineer, a.k.a Tone Deaf, for his sterling work twiddling knobs every night and for also working the mixing desk. Tony has a rare knack of turning a pristine, beautiful note into screeching feedback. His addition of distortion to the opening bars of "Maybe Tomorrow" a sad, mournful, acoustic ballad, gives the song a new context I'd never envisaged or intended. And lastly, his skilful use of the "muffle" button on every song is a joy to behold.

Another big thank you to our two guitar techs, Stevie and Joe—a.k.a. Club Foot and Cack Hand. Their ability to drop, bang, damage and lose guitars is revered throughout the music industry. This sort of talent is not learnt overnight. It takes years of experience and unrelenting non-thinking to achieve this level of skill. A special mention must go to Cack Hand, who has broken the laws of western musical notation that have been in force for millennia. He has found a new musical note. I'm a bit of a stickler for the established conventions of standard tuning, so I was wary at first when he tuned my G string to H.

But, as he persisted in doing it for every single gig, "H" has grown on me somewhat, if not the audience.

And what would we have done without Ricky Jones our very own Cable Guy. Broken leads, dodgy cables, dead microphones, buzzing pickups, smoking amplifiers, you name it and he can cause it. Being repeatedly zapped on the lip by a badly earthed microphone was a tad annoying at first. But as the tour progressed, and the shocks increased in ferocity, I almost began to look forward to them—a bit like a masochist looks forward to a spell in the dungeon.

And then there's Billy, our lighting man, a.k.a. lights on but no-one's home. I have already made an appointment to see (or not) a Harley Street eye specialist as soon as this tour is over. His predilection for the strobe light is to be commended. I believe he broke a world record at the Leeds gig when fifteen epileptics had to be treated by the paramedics. Keep up the good work Billy and may the lights never go out... as they did at Cardiff!

And last but not least, a very special thank you to "Bong" our drum tech. As you all know, Bong is from Somerset so doesn't speak English but he is fluent in "Grunt", the universal language of roadies. Is there anyone in the world who can change a torn drum skin or fix a loose drum pedal faster than Bong? Well, the obvious answer is "yes". In fact, I believe my Doberman Pinscher could adjust a drum stool quicker than Bong, but it's a rather unfair comparison as we all know how intelligent Doberman Pinschers are.

To you all, we love you and admire you and long may the grunting continue. Cheers!'

⋙ ⋘

It is the end of the Resurrection Tour. I've been praying for the end to come, but now it's here I feel a little melancholy. We've had some ups and downs, some highs and lows, but we made it through relatively unscathed. I forgot how gruelling being on the road can be, and I'm not sure this is the life for me anymore. I must finish now, as I've just seen Geordie pick Flaky up by the throat—never a good sign—although perfectly understandable.

Keep On Keeping On - *Will Harding*

Thank You For Reading

I hope you enjoyed **The Tour Diaries,** and here's an interesting fact. The diaries were initially intended to be part of my first book in the series, Arc Of A Shooting Star, which starts with Will, alone in self-imposed isolation. It charts the story of how he reformed his band and headed out on the Resurrection Tour. However, as that book was a whopping 140k words long, I decided to pull the Tour Diaries from it and offer it up as a short story in the series.

If you'd like to go back to the beginning then here's a link to **Arc Of A Shooting Star**. Alternatively, the later books can be read in any order and my latest one is **Eggs Unscrambled**. This involves our hapless gang, and their families, going on a camping holiday together, with some unpredictable results.

Let's Keep In Touch

If you wish to keep up to date with my book news, there are a few simple ways to be notified. You can subscribe to my entertaining (subjective) monthly "**Discombobulated**" newsletter. This not only keeps you abreast of new releases, but occasionally I have a free book to giveaway or promotional discounts. The newsletter is designed to entertain, with short, pithy takes on the world and life... mostly my life. There's no hard sell and I won't be inundating you with spammy "buy, buy, buy" nonsense – which I personally detest. You can sign up by following the link below, which will take you to my website.

I would like to subscribe to your newsletter.

Alternatively, you can go to the following sites and click on the "**Follow**" button.

BookBub

Amazon

Facebook

For paperback readers, the links above won't work no matter how many times you tap your finger on the paper. Below is a manual link to type into your browser.

https://www.subscribepage.com/author_simon_northouse_home

If you enjoyed this book, then all **reviews** are greatly appreciated.

To contact me, my email address is:

simon@simonnorthouse.com

I enjoy a chat, and will always reply.

Also By Simon Northouse

The Shooting Star Series

Arc Of A Shooting Star (Novel)

The Resurrection Tour Diaries (Short Story)

Catch A Shooting Star (Novel)

Fall Of A Shooting Star (Novel)

What's It All About... Geordie? (Novel)

Nuts At Christmas (Novella)

Eggs Unscrambled (Novel)

I Will Survive (Novel)

Bells At New Year (Novel) – November 2021

The Soul Love Series

Soul Love (Prequel Novella)

Love Is The Goal (Novel)

Love On A Roll (Novel)

Love Of The Coal (Novel) - December 2021

The Discombobulated Newsletter Series

Keep On Keeping On (Novella)

Keep Karma and Carry On (Novella)

The Lockdown Diary Blues (Novella)

Keep On Keeping On Again! (Novella) - July 2021

❦

The School Days Series

The School Report - Before We Were Tsars (Novella)

The School Report - The Final Term (Novella)